THE BROKEN MAN

THE TRAVELS OF JACOB WOLF

STEVEN E. WEDEL

MOONHOWLER PRESS

The author humbly dedicates this book to the memory of David R. Lewis, whose writing, life, and joy are an inspiration that was discovered almost too late. It was an honor to correspond with you, sir. We'll meet in person on the other side.

Contents

FOREWORD

My name is Jacob Wolf and these are the stories of my life. I figure I should tell them myself before some damn fool back East tries to make me out to be some kind of dime-novel hero like Bill Cody. It ain't like that. I ain't no hero. I'm just an old man who started out as a dumb young kid and survived, more by luck than anything else. These stories are true, but like every story, they're only true if you see them through my eyes.

1

———•———

GREEN AS SUMMER GRASS

"That rig yer wearin' looks new. You ever drawed down on a man before?"

I looked over at the man on my right. He'd introduced himself as John Kepford and I told him my name, Jacob Wolf. He was wearing dirty chambray pants and a shirt that had been red once but the front was slick and brown with grime and the sleeves had rips and little patches in various colors. I knew he'd sewed those patches on himself because they were sloppy. His hat had a couple of holes in the crown and the brim was rolled on the left side. He hadn't shaved in a while, but the hair on his face couldn't rightly be called a beard. "I don't think you need the answer to that," I finally said to him.

John Kepford wasn't the first bully I'd encountered in my life, but he was the first of my new life, the life I'd chosen when I left San Antonio behind me for a life of wandering. A new life, certain death, and hopefully enough glory to break a heart.

"Yer either green as summer grass, or somebody stol't your rig and you had to buy a new one," Kepford said. "I'm thinking you ain't been north of the Brazos more'n a couple of days."

Kepford had ridden up on me shortly after sunrise, claiming he saw the smoke of a breakfast fire that must have been big enough to roast a

Kiowa brave over. He asked which way I was going, and when I vaguely said, "West," Kepford said we were going the same way and might as well ride together. He'd been jogging along on his bay mare ever since, his mouth seldom stopping.

"I know what I'm doing," I told him.

"Do ya?" Kepford gave me a knowing look that traveled over me and my horse, then he told me what he saw. "Yer a young fella on a swayback ol' mare that prolly still dreams of pulling a plow up until her last owner sold her to you for double her value. That saddle was old when Lee surrendered. You ain't got no rifle, nor even a shotgun on you. Yer clothes are dusty, but clean, and like I was saying, the leather of that pistol holster looks like it was on a store shelf a few days ago."

I looked at the other man again, but I didn't say anything. He was right about everything he said, but I wasn't going to admit it.

"What'd ya do afore you came out west?" Kepford asked.

I thought back to my long days in the general store, stocking shelves and dusting and mopping floors and ... And Rebecca. I remembered stealing the Colt .44 revolver with the holster and cartridge belt and five boxes of ammunition and running through the night away from that life. "I had a job," I said.

Kepford pulled out a plug of tobacco and cut off a piece, lipping it off the side of his folding knife. He didn't offer me any, but put the plug and knife away as his grizzled chin began working the tobacco. He spat. "Had me a job in a livery stable once," he said. "That what you did?"

"No," I answered.

"I got caught in the loft with the owner's wife," Kepford laughed. "You ever punch a pissed off husband with yer pants down and yer hard pecker swingin' around?"

"No," I answered again.

"Knocked him out, then finished up with his wife, but figgered my employment was over, ya know? I picked me out the best horse and moseyed along."

I gave the man a glance and found Kepford was looking back at me, grinning. I started to turn my head back to the west, wondering how I was going to get rid of my unwanted companion, and that's when I saw his partner trailing along behind us. He was still pretty far back and I only got a glimpse of him out of the tail of my eye. I pretended I hadn't seen him and turned back to the waving grass in front of us.

"Some folks'd tell you it's dangerous for one man to be travelin' alone out here. 'Specially fer a greenhorn."

"Do you really think my gun looks too new?" I asked, and clumsily pulled it from the shiny black leather holster. The clumsiness was less of an act than I would have liked, but I was as young and green as my unwanted company said I was. I'd done some practicing with that gun and I got to where I could shoot a tree trunk from about fifty paces if I took careful aim and a few deep, calming breaths. Tree trunks don't shoot back, though.

Kepford laughed and mockingly held up his hands, the reins dangling between the fingers of his left. "Don't shoot me, pardner," he teased.

I pretended to study the blue-black barrel of my revolver. "I haven't shot it much," I confessed. "I grew up in Kentucky. There was a girl, and her folks decided to move west. I thought we were going to get married, so I left my ma and pa and followed her." I looked up from the gun to meet Kepford's dark, laughing eyes.

"She die?" he asked.

"To me she did," I answered. "You make me remember a lesson from my schoolhouse days back in Kentucky. Miss Laura was teaching us something about the slave days, and she told us about something called 'moral ambiguity.' You ever heard of that?"

"Nope," Kepford said, and now he openly looked over my shoulder at his partner in the distance. "What's it mean?"

"Well, you plan to rob me and probably kill me with your friend, but so far you haven't threatened me," I told him. Now his dark eyes were hard on me. "You haven't made no threat yet, but ..."

I shot him then.

I knew in that heartbeat that I'd made a mistake and was lucky for the moment. My eyes gave me away, I guess, because between pulling back the hammer on that Colt and pulling the trigger, he knew what I was about to do and he went for his gun.

My bullet hit Kepford in the chest. I saw a spot of blood appear as his horse reared. Kepford slid out of the saddle and hit the ground. Hoofbeats were approaching fast from behind and to my left as my own old plow horse danced under me. I jumped out of the old saddle and let the horse hurry away.

Rebecca's face flashed through my mind, the way she had looked at me early on, when she'd promised we had a future together. Then I remembered her final words to me, carried in my shirt pocket, and my own resolve to make her sorry she'd sent me away. Time seemed to slow and I felt my body grow cold. My concentration focused on the man riding toward me.

Life and death don't matter much after your heart is ripped out.

The man approaching was fat and as grimy looking as Kepford himself. He was yelling as he bounced in the saddle of his galloping horse. He had his pistol out and he fired three shots at me. Two hit the ground yards in front of me and the third went wide to my right. When he was about thirty yards away, I raised my Colt and fired back at the man. My first shot missed, but his horse reared. The rider stopped and his mount skittered to the side as the rider slapped and fought to control the animal. I aimed again, looking at the man's chest and thinking of a tree trunk, but the shot was high. The rider's head seemed to explode.

The fat man hit the earth, pulling his horse down on top of him. The horse rolled to its feet and shook itself, tossed its head, then galloped away, toward the two other horses standing close by eating grass.

A shot rang out behind me and I felt something tug at my shirt sleeve. I turned and found John Kepford on his belly, his right arm extended toward me, the gun trembling in his hand. "You goddamn pup," he shouted through bloody teeth, then he fired again.

He missed.

I didn't.

My bullet didn't take him in the head like I'd planned, but hit him in the right shoulder. He screamed and dropped his gun as his face contorted in pain. Keeping my own gun in my hand, I walked over and looked down at him.

"You were going to rob and kill me, weren't you?" I asked.

Kepford moaned and held a hand over his bleeding shoulder. He turned angry, scared eyes up to me. "We prolly wouldn't a kilt ya," he admitted.

"Adultery, horse stealing, attempted robbery, and you didn't rule out murder," I said. "Who knows what other crimes you're guilty of?" I remember I looked up at the vast pale blue sky over Texas. There isn't anything I've come across in all my years that'll remind a man of just how small and insignificant he is as miles of prairie under a cloudless blue sky. "I guess this is for the best."

I shot John Kepford in the forehead, then took the few coins the man and his friend had in their pockets, unsaddled Kepford's horse and my old nag and turned them loose. Kepford's friend had a nice, new-looking Winchester repeating rifle, the kind called a Yellowboy, and I took that and all the cartridges I could find.

Did that make me a thief? Did shooting Kepford before he had a fair chance to go for his weapon make me a murderer? Was I just as bad as them, but luckier?

That was a long time ago and I still don't know the answer. I reckon it's for God to decide. I expect we'll talk it over when I go to see Him.

I mounted my new stallion, a spirited black with one white foot and a white blaze on his forehead, and set off in a lope, reloading my pistol as I rode northwest. The coyotes and buzzards could have what I'd left behind.

2

Questions from a Sheriff

The next day, I was in a saloon in a little town on the bank of Salt Creek. I was standing with my back to the bar, drinking a glass of warm beer while I listened to four men argue over a game of cards. It was the usual thing about the number of aces or kings in the deck. It was new to me then and I was trying to decide if things were going to turn into a fight.

"Hey, cowboy. Buy a girl a drink?"

A woman had moved up next to me at the bar. She was short, with brown curls framing a delicate face made up with wet red lipstick. Her brown eyes twinkled as she looked up at me and smiled with perfect teeth. Her shoulders were white as milk. Her green dress was tight on the top, cut low to show mounds of soft breasts that seemed to have a life of their own as she breathed. Her skirt rustled when she lifted a foot to the rail at the bottom of the bar. She cocked her head. "Well?" she asked.

"Yes, ma'am," I said. I waved the bartender over and he took a different bottle from beneath the bar and poured the woman a drink, then replaced the bottle. "Do ladies get the better whiskey?" I asked her.

She laughed as she lifted the glass and swirled the amber liquid. "Gus just knows what I like," she said. She took a sip, her eyes never leaving my face as she raised the glass. She lowered it and asked, "Where are you from, cowboy?"

"Somewhere else," I said. "And I'm no cowboy." I didn't want her there. I didn't want to talk to a woman, but my ma raised me right and I couldn't be rude.

"We're all from somewhere else," she said. "Most of us, anyway. I'm from Kansas City. I've been here almost a year. So, where are you from?"

The men at the table dealt a new hand of cards, the curses simmering to low growls interrupted by gulps of whiskey or beer and requests for more cards or placed bets. The man with his back to me was trying a bluff while holding a pair of threes, a queen, a ten, and an ace.

"I was born in Kentucky," I told the whore. "I came to Texas about a year ago."

"You been working for a rancher?" she asked. The lights of the candles burning above us made her eyes shine. She was pretty, but she was wasting her time.

"No, ma'am," I answered. "I was a clerk in a store until pretty recently."

"You don't look like no store clerk," she said, looking me up and down. She finally came to her point. "How would you like a little company tonight?"

"No, ma'am," I told her. "I've had my fill of women."

She laughed. "I think you – "

The noise of the saloon went suddenly quiet. A big man had entered the bar and stood just inside the door, looking the place over, a silver star glinting on his chest. He was over six feet tall with shoulders like an ox and gray eyes made of cold steel under a sweat-stained brown hat. There were a few nervous murmured greetings before the bartender called out to the man.

"What can I do for you, Sheriff?"

"Who's riding the black stallion with the white sock?" the sheriff asked.

There was more murmuring, then an older man near the far wall stood up. "I gotta black gelding with a white sock."

The sheriff gave him a quick glance, then looked away. "I know a set of balls when I see one," he said. "White blaze on its face."

By this time, my insides were crawling around under my skin. I didn't have any paperwork to show that was my horse. Kepford's friend probably stole the horse before I killed him and took it for myself. How would I prove that, though? Would it even matter?

I saw a couple of cowboys who'd come into the saloon behind me glancing my way and I knew if they spoke first I'd be in worse shape, so I pushed away from the bar and faced the lawman. I won't lie to you, my heart was probably visible between my teeth when I spoke up.

"I rode it," I admitted.

"Is it yours?" he demanded.

I looked away, then back at the man. "The fella riding him before me didn't need him anymore."

"Because you killed him?" The man's eyes were like knives driving into me, holding me in place. I swallowed hard and nodded once.

"I killed him," I said.

"You better come with me," the sheriff said.

He stood there, waiting, and I had no choice but to go to him. I felt the eyes of the whore on me as I moved away and I think there was admiration there. Women are strange creatures. Nobody spoke as I walked. People who were standing stepped away to let me pass. When

I got to the sheriff, he turned sideways and motioned toward the door, so I left the saloon and he came out behind him.

"I guess you'll want my gun," I said, reaching for the butt of my revolver.

"Are you gonna shoot me?" the lawman asked.

"No, sir," I answered.

"Then just keep it. For now," he said. "My office is across the street. Let's go."

There were three horses tied to the post outside the sheriff's office. I recognized two of them. One was the old mare I had ridden away from San Antonio and the other had belonged to Kepford. Kepford was draped over the back of my mare and his partner was hanging over Kepford's horse, both tied in place. The third horse was a huge black stallion that stamped a hind leg as we came up, giving me the idea he was impatient about something. I swear, that was the biggest horse I've ever seen, right up to this day.

"You know these men?" the sheriff asked, pausing on the boardwalk in front of his office.

"Yeah," I said drily.

"You killed them?"

"I did," I confessed. In my mind, I saw thick rock walls and prison bars and years and years of my life slipping away from me. Or maybe they'd just hang me. That thought was comforting. "They tried to rob me, though."

The sheriff only nodded, then opened the door of his office. "Come on in and tell me about it."

The office was brightly lit with an oil lamp. There was a heavy desk, a rack with a couple of rifles and a long-tom shotgun. Two wooden chairs sat in front of the desk and a tall-backed leather swivel chair behind the desk. A pot-bellied stove gave off a little heat in a corner by the window and a half-open door showed a series of cells down a dim hallway. The sheriff dropped into the leather chair and motioned me toward one of the chairs on the other side of the desk.

"What's your name?" he asked me.

"Jacob Wolf," I said.

"Where'd you come from, Jacob Wolf?" I was reminded of the whore's questions.

"I grew up in Kentucky," I repeated. "Came out west about a year ago. To San Antonio."

"What brings you up this way?" he asked, then grinned at me. "Other than that stallion?"

I was dumbfounded for a minute, wondering what he meant, then I got that he'd made a joke. I smiled nervously, but the whole time I was wondering if that was a good sign, or if he was playing with me like a barn cat plays with a mouse.

"I … was looking for a new life," I said.

"What'd you do in San Antone?"

I had to look down at my hands in my lap. "Worked as a clerk in a hardware store."

"Why'd you leave that?"

It was here that I deviated from the truth. Even though this big, hard-eyed man was the law, there were some things I just didn't want to talk to him about. "Working in a store wasn't what I wanted to do. I saved up some money and bought that old mare outside and rode off."

"Uh-huh. And what were you gonna do next?" he asked. His eyes were fixed on me, but the hardness wasn't so severe. "You didn't plan to become a gunfighter, did you?"

I shook my head and returned to the truth. "I don't know," I said. "I just had to get away."

"From trouble?" The eyes sharpened a little.

"No," I answered. "Not trouble. Just somebody I didn't want to be around anymore."

He nodded. "Okay. Tell me how you came to be in possession of that fine stallion."

I told him the whole story, from the time Kepford rode up until I'd shot him and his partner. "I'd figured out that the old mare I was riding wasn't much of a horse," I said. "I really didn't know anything when I bought her. She's a good horse, but not fast and doesn't want to go all day. Those fellas didn't need their horses, so I took the one I could catch and rode away."

The sheriff's eyes left my face and looked over my left shoulder. Before I could turn my head, a thick, deep voice spoke. "That's purty much how it seemed to me."

3

A PARTNERSHIP FORMED

Leaning against the door frame leading to the cells was the largest man I'd ever seen. He filled the doorway from the floor to the top of the frame, and side to side at the shoulder. He wore black boots, black pants, a crimson shirt, black vest, orange kerchief, and black Stetson hat. His skin was almost as black as the coat of the stallion I'd claimed. His eyes were fixed on me and his teeth flashed in a smile.

"That was some good shootin'," the black man said. "You dinnit get hit nowhere?"

"No," I said, shaking my head. "A bullet tore my shirt a little." I showed him where the bullet had narrowly missed my arm. He clucked his tongue and shook his head.

"Jacob Wolf, this is Jerome Freeman," the sheriff said. "He's a bounty hunter. He found the bodies you left out there."

"Nice reward for both of 'em," Jerome Freeman added.

The sheriff nodded. "They're part of a gang that's been been terrorizing the roads and trails around here for a while now, going after people like you, traveling alone, or families that weren't armed."

"If ev'rything happened jus' like you said, you must be one cool hand with a gun," Jerome Freeman said.

"It happened the way I said," I snapped at him, my dander rising over him maybe saying I wasn't telling the truth.

The bounty hunter held up two hands the size of skillets and smiled at me. "I ain't saying it didn't. Just that it took a lotta guts to open up on two experienced gun hands like those rascals. I was plannin' to take 'em from ambush, myself."

"I didn't have much of a choice," I answered. "When I saw that fat one coming up on us, I knew for sure what was about to happen." I paused, thinking, then asked, "Were they killing people? Or just robbing them?"

The sheriff rubbed at his chin. "That makes a difference to you?"

"It's something I've had on my mind," I admitted.

He nodded. "Mostly robbing, but anyone who fought back, or even looked like they were about to, got shot. And then there was the Peters girl." He hesitated, looked up at the bounty hunter, then me. I sensed I was the only one who didn't know. "Didn't kill her, but they both had their way with her before letting her go."

"I guess they deserved it then," I said quietly. It gave me a good piece of satisfaction to know they were real bad men.

"I can have the reward money here tomorrow," the sheriff said. "The question is, who do I give it to?"

"I did bring them in," Jerome Freeman said.

"But young Jacob here took all the risk," the sheriff told him. He gave me a look that said I should speak up.

"I didn't kill them for any reward. I didn't know anything about that. I was just trying to stay alive," I said.

"But it gives you a claim on the money," the sheriff said.

"Brad, are you tryin' to give my money away?" Jerome asked.

"I'm gauging this young man's character," the sheriff said. "Why don't you sit your black ass down so I don't have to look up so high to talk to you?"

The bounty hunter chuckled and pulled back the chair beside me to lower himself into it. The wood creaked under his weight. "You think I need to give him half the money," Freeman said.

"I think it would be the right thing to do," the sheriff said. "If I'm guessing right, his pockets probably aren't full of jack." He looked at me.

"I have a little," I said. It was damn little, mostly made up of the coins I'd taken from the dead men.

"I'm thinking you two could help each other out," the sheriff continued. "Jacob, can you read and write?"

"Yes, sir," I answered.

"How much schooling do you have?"

"My mama made me finish eighth grade," I said. "That's as high as our school went."

The sheriff swiveled his chair to face the giant next to me. "Who's reading the wanted posters for you these days?" he asked.

Jerome Freeman's humor was gone. He shrugged his massive shoulders and looked at his lap. "I finds somebody."

"I hope they're more trustworthy than the one who told you old Ben Miller was a horse thief," the sheriff said.

"Ah, now, Sheriff, I knowed you was about to bring that up," Freeman said, and now he was grinning again, but it was a sheepish grin.

"You couldn't read the name on the poster you had for Bart Sampson and you couldn't read the bill of sale Ben had for those horses," the sheriff said. "Jacob here's a young fella with no job. He's drifting, and he's good with a gun. If he gets in with the wrong people, he'll go bad. You could teach him your trade, and he can help you out with reading and writing when you need to."

"Who said I wanted to be a bounty hunter?" I broke in. I thought this sheriff had a hell of a lot of nerve setting me up for a future I had never even considered.

"You know I ain't never had a partner, Brad," Freeman said.

"I do know it. And I know some of the trouble you have in your job," the sheriff said. "Not just with the reading. Lots of folks have a real problem with a black man gunning down white men for money. If you have a white partner, a lot of that will go away."

"I said I never said I wanted to be a bounty hunter," I protested again, my voice a little hotter than before. The sheriff turned his gaze back to me and now his eyes were hard and cold again.

"You're not a vagrant in my town, are you?" he asked.

"I only got here today," I complained. "I don't aim to stay here."

"Have you rented a room in a hotel? Do you have livery for your horse?" the sheriff asked me. "By the way, that horse might be stolen. I'll have to check on that. It won't look good if you're in possession of a stolen horse. Or in jail for vagrancy."

"What the hell is this?" I asked.

"I agree with him," Freeman said. "It looks like you're railroading us together whether we want each other or not. I don't know nothing about this boy. Is he stupid? No offense, young fella, but I don't know. I don't want to get kilt out there because of him."

"Then you better train him well," the sheriff said. "From what he's told us here today, he seems to be a young man of integrity and education who can think quickly and act like he needs to in a tight spot. He might save your ass a time or two."

"You gonna bring that up, too?" Freeman asked. The sheriff grinned. I looked from one to the other.

"Somebody shot you in the ass?" I asked Freeman.

"Twice," the sheriff answered for him.

"Three times," Freeman grumbled. "But I guess that once was more in the thigh."

"You're lucky to still be alive," the sheriff told him. "You need a partner." He looked at me. "And you need a job. I get the feeling you don't wanna be tied down as, say, a clerk in a hardware store."

"No," I admitted.

"This could be a good opportunity for you," the sheriff said.

"I get the feeling I'll be arrested if I say no," I told him.

He grinned. "You've got money coming to you in the morning, assuming you and Jerome here are agreeable about splitting that reward money for Callahan and Kepford."

"Ain't you busy enough around here, Brad?" Freeman asked. "How long you been sitting around in this office cookin' up this partnership?"

"Made it up on the spot," the sheriff said. "I got a mind like a steel trap."

"And we's the ones trapped in it," Freeman said. "Can me and the boy at least talk this thing over amongst ourselves? We might not even like each other."

"Of course you can," the sheriff said, grinning with satisfaction. "It's a free country."

Jerome Freeman grunted. "So, you's gonna back me up if we go over to the saloon where you found him?"

The sheriff's smile fell away and for the first time he looked away. "I wish I could, Jerome." He picked at a nick on the edge of his desk, then looked up at us again. "How about this? I'll have dinner and a bottle sent over and you two just use my office. I need to make my rounds through the town and stay in the saloons for a while to make sure everything is calm. Will that work?"

"That works for me, boss," Jerome said.

The sheriff looked at me and I shrugged. "Yes, sir," I said. "How much will that cost?"

He waved my question away. "It's on the sheriff's office today," he said. He pushed himself out of his swivel chair, the leather creaking as he left it. He adjusted his gun holster, promised to be back soon, and left us alone in the office.

"Well, young Jacob Wolf, what do you think about all of this?" Jerome Freeman asked me.

I scraped my chair over the rough boards of the floor to turn and face the giant of a man. He turned his chair a little, too. "Why is he doing this?" I asked.

"Sheriff Brad Harrison is a good man," Freeman said. "I'm sure he thinks this is a good idea."

"Is it?" I asked.

Freeman shrugged his huge shoulders. "It could be. But it might not be. Depends on how we get on, I reckon. Are you an agreeable type of person?"

"I think so," I said.

"You got any bad habits?" he asked. "Drinkin'? Whorin'? Gamblin'?"

"I'll have a drink sometimes," I told him.

"You tell me, Jacob Wolf," he said. "Do you wanna do this? You wanna learn how to be a bounty hunter?"

I thought about it. At the time, you see, I didn't know anything about the profession. My feet were as tender as Ma's Sunday roast beef. I knew I didn't want to work in a store. I had something driving me that I didn't want to talk about yet, and maybe would never want to talk about. That's what I thought then. But also, I knew I needed to do something to earn money. I wasn't so green that I thought I could just live off the fat of the land.

"What would I have to do?" I asked.

"Follow directions from me, mostly," Freeman said. "You ever took orders from a black man afore?"

"No."

"You got a problem with it?"

I shrugged. "You're the expert."

"I tells you to go left and hide behind a log, you'll do it?" he asked. I nodded. "I tells you to guard prisoners while I sleep, you'll do it?" I nodded again. "I tells you to put a shine on my boots, you'll do it?"

"You can shine your own damn boots," I said hotly.

Freeman's huge face split into that big white grin and he chuckled at me. "Good," he said. "You seem reasonable enough."

"What about you?" I asked. "What kind of man are you on the trail?"

He shrugged his shoulders and turned his palms up. "I mostly been traveling alone. When I know I ain't near to the people I'm trackin', I might sing a little. I make a damn fine pot of coffee. Once I'm closin' in on my bounty, though, I'm all business. They ain't no playin' around when the bullets might be about to fly."

I nodded my understanding.

"Brad, he gonna hound us until we agree to what he wants," Freeman told me. "We might as well agree to at least travel out of here together. We can see how it goes after that. You agreeable?"

"What about the bounties?" I asked. "Whoever shoots them gets the money?"

He laughed deep down in his belly, his cheeks rising up, his teeth blazing white and his pink tongue visible behind them. "No, boy.

Sometimes the law wants us to bring people back alive. I don't always do those jobs, but if the pay is good, then I might. You do your share, do like I tells ya, I'm willing to be fair with ya."

"What's fair?" I asked. "Half?"

He gave me a side-eye. "Half is a lot when I don't know if you'll be any damn good to me yet."

"I want half," I said firmly. "I killed Kepford and what's-his-name by myself."

"You did. You did," Freeman agreed. "That other fell's name is Simon Callahan. And what I saw from the tracks, it looks like it happened like you said. But how do I know that wasn't a piece of luck?"

I thought about that. He had a point, and I honestly couldn't argue in favor of my skill as a killer. If Kepford had caught on a second earlier that I wasn't just showing him my pistol, he would have had time to draw and kill me. Still, I felt like I should hold my ground. "If we're partners, we should split everything evenly," I said.

"I think it's more like you'll be my apprentice first," Freeman said. "You gotta learn the ropes. They ain't a lot of rules to bein' a bounty hunter, but they is some. And they's some tricks that'll keep you alive. Some folks just plum don't wanna get taken to jail or shot. How about you get a fourth until I think you've graduated from bein' a apprentice?"

I knew his offer was fair, but didn't want to admit it. "Do you know math?" I asked him.

"I knows a little, but I'll have to rely on your schoolin' and honesty," Freeman said. He said it soberly, but with a hint of friendliness. Warmth. I was starting to like this giant of a man.

"Then I guess you have a deal," I said.

"Fine. That's fine," he said. "Now where's that sheriff and our dinner?"

4

CONFESSION

Within a few minutes, there was a knock at the door of the office. It was a light knock, not the kind made by the firm, bold hand of Sheriff Brad Harrison. I was closer to the door, so I got up to open it. There was a woman in a blue calico dress on the other side. Her dark hair was pulled back into a tight knot and her face tilted up to look at me. Brown eyes flashed as she took in my features.

"Sheriff asked me to bring dinner over," she announced.

I looked down at her empty hands.

"It's on this here chair," she said as if explaining the obvious to a fool. "I couldn't very well hold it and knock on the door." She turned and bent to pick up a wooden tray stacked with covered dishes. She handed the heavy tray to me, adding, "I'll be wanting all of that back when you're finished."

"Yes, ma'am," I said.

"The sheriff already paid for it," she announced, then spun on her heel and marched away, her skirt swishing around her legs.

I carried the tray to the desk and set it down. "I wonder if the service is better in the café," I said.

Jerome Freeman chuckled. "Probably woulda been a lot worse ifen I'da opened the door," he said.

We were uncovering plates and taking in the sights and smells of steaks and fried potatoes, green beans, fresh bread, and apple pie. "Why's that?" I asked.

"Boy, are you really that dumb to the way things are?" he asked.

I felt my blood warm up at that and my hands tightened on my plate. I wondered if I was going to have to draw on this giant of a man, and whether or not I had a chance of winning that contest. I figured they were non-existent to not-good, and being gunned down by a bounty hunter who probably didn't even realize he'd offended me wasn't how I wanted to go.

"Listen, Mr. Freeman," I began. "I've been played for a fool and I don't plan for it to happen again. I don't appreciate you calling me dumb. If you're saying the issue is the fact that you're black, I don't understand. I've seen lots of black men with whites and Mexicans working on ranches here in Texas."

Jerome Freeman sat very still while I spoke, his silver fork hovering over his plate. When he was satisfied that I was finished, he pointed the tines of the fork at me and asked, "How many a them you see inside a place that serves white folk? They come into the store where you use ta work?"

"Well ... no," I admitted.

"You see 'em treated with respect by little white gals like the one that brought this here food?"

"No," I answered sheepishly.

"You've seen cowhands ridin' through streets somewhere. That's all. Maybe them white folks don't think much about ridin' with black men, but they prolly don't like it none. That's just the way it is."

I nodded.

Jerome lowered his fork and took up a knife to cut into his steak. He looked up at me again and grinned. "But I like the way you think 'bout things. And you called me Mr. Freeman, just like if I was a respectable lawyer or somethin'. I could get used to that. But you better not do it. White folks'd have a fit. You just call me Jerome."

My mouth was watering over the smell of the food, but I was finding myself liking this huge, no-nonsense, worldly man. And I was feeling more than a little guilty. I cut a piece off my own steak and chewed it a little. "Jerome?" I asked.

"Yeah?" he asked, his mouth full.

"It was luck."

His ten-gallon jaw stopped chewing for just a heartbeat, then he finished and swallowed and nodded, his teeth showing in another grin. "I figgered that much," he said.

"Kepford knew I was green and he was making fun of me and I saw his partner coming up behind us," I confessed. "I took out my gun like I barely knew how to draw it and was looking at it and he was joking about me shooting him. And then I just did. In the chest, but it didn't kill him. It took three shots to kill his partner, and then I had to put two more into Kepford."

The whole time I spilled this story, Jerome Freeman sat rock-still with his knife and fork poised over his plate, but his full, very serious attention, was on me. When he knew I was finished, he nodded his head. "I'm glad you tol' me," he said. "We'll hafta work on your accuracy."

"You don't want to call this all off?" I asked.

"Nah," he said and grinned again. He stabbed a mess of green beans with his fork. "You got lucky, but you made a plan when you was in a tight spot and you didn't panic when they started shootin' back at ya. That usually only comes with experience. Lots of it. Now shut the hell up and let a man eat afore this food gets cold."

We ate then without talking anymore. The food was real good and I was glad to have it. I'm not the best cook on the trail, so I mostly eat jerky and corn dodgers. We finished the meal and Jerome suggested I take the dishes back over to the café.

"So's the li'l gal don' get worried the giant Negro stole't 'em," he said.

It wasn't something I wanted to do, but I did it. The restaurant was about half full and lots of folks looked up when I went inside. The smell of all that food was so strong and so good it almost made me hungry again. The girl who'd brought us our food came over and I handed the stack of plates and cups over to her.

"How can you eat with him?" she asked in a hiss of a whisper.

"Who?" I asked.

"That … darky," she answered.

"He's just a fella, ma'am," I said. I tipped my hat and thanked her, then hurried out of there.

I've been around lots of folks who didn't like black people back home. After the war and the slaves all got their freedom, a lot of white people hated them even more than when they were slaves. The black people I knew were always nice enough. They usually treated me better than rich white folks who thought they were better than me and the poor white trash that thought I was putting on airs because Ma made me finish school and I talked better than them.

When I opened the door to the sheriff's office I found that Sheriff Brad Harrison had returned. He and Jerome Freeman had uncorked a whiskey bottle and the sheriff was pouring the amber fluid into three glasses.

"I assumed a stone-cold killer like you drank whiskey," the sheriff said.

"Of course," I answered. I preferred a cold beer, but now didn't seem the time to mention that.

"The sheriff here has a job for us," Jerome said as he raised a glass at me.

5

"Do This One for Me"

The whiskey was warm and strong. I sipped at mine, while the older men took it in gulps and refilled their glasses, ignoring the fact I wasn't keeping up. The sheriff was back behind his desk. Jerome and I sat in the chairs we'd been in while we ate. There were a few long sheets of thick paper on the sheriff's desk.

Jerome tipped his glass toward the lawman but spoke to me. "Ol' Sheriff Harrison here wants us to ketch the rest of the band robbin' folks comin' into town."

"Isn't that the job of the law?" I asked.

"I'm a town sheriff," the lawman explained. "I don't have any jurisdiction beyond the borders of the town, so even if I found these guys, I couldn't arrest them. Unless they do something in town and I chase them out and catch them that way, but if they're coming into this town, they're not being seen by me."

"What about a marshal or the Texas Rangers?" I asked.

"There hasn't been a United States marshal pass through here for a few years," Sheriff Harrison said. "And the Rangers are all busy somewhere else. There are raids from Mexico and some Comanche trouble further west." He put his glass to his lips and threw his head back to catch the last of the whiskey in it. He swallowed and banged the glass down on the table. "There just ain't enough lawmen to keep up with the bandits, rustlers, and murderers."

"Can't you deputize some men?" I asked.

The sheriff eyed me as if I was daft. "Even if I could find some men willing to be shot at, there's still the jurisdiction problem," he said.

"Oh. Yeah," I acknowledged.

"That's what keeps us workin', young Jake," Jerome said. "If every law office was done filled up with lawmen, wouldn't be no need of us."

"I guess not," I said. "So, what do we do? Go arrest those guys? How many of them are there?"

"Listen to him," Jerome teased. He swirled the whiskey in his glass and grinned at the sheriff. "He talks like it's the easiest thing in the world to bring fugitives to justice."

"Well, to be fair, those last two didn't give him much trouble," Sheriff Harrison answered thoughtfully, but I knew he was playing, too. I decided to go along with them.

"You just make them think you're dumb, then shoot them," I said. "If I can do it, you two sure can." That last line kind of slipped out before I really thought about it and once it was out there I was pretty worried the two men would get mad at me. Instead, they laughed so hard that I had to wonder just how much whiskey they'd drunk.

"He's got some spunk," the sheriff said to my new partner.

When they stopped laughing, the sheriff lifted two wanted posters from his desk and handed them to me. One featured a rough-looking man who appeared to be maybe just over thirty years old named Albert Dewey. He had a dull scar on his cheek, black hair, a stubbled face, and dark eyes in the drawing. There was a $500 reward for his capture. The other poster was for a young man, probably about my own age of eighteen, with light hair and high cheekbones. His name was David Buckles and he was worth $200.

"They were last seen west of town," Harrison said. "Two days ago they robbed a farmer on his way home. He'd spent all his money, so they roughed him up and destroyed most of the supplies he'd bought. They'll usually lay low for a week or so after a successful robbery, make people think maybe they've left the area, then strike again. They might not wait this time."

"They were working with those two I shot?" I asked.

"I think so. Sometimes two would work the east road and two the west. Sometimes all four would work together," the sheriff said.

"Do it say dead or alive on there somewhere?" Jerome asked, craning his neck to see the posters I held.

"No," Harrison answered. "Besides these robberies, they're both wanted for questioning in separate killings, but they need to be brought in alive if at all possible."

Jerome clicked his tongue and shook his head slowly. "You know I like when I have the option to bring 'em back cold," he said.

"I know," the sheriff said. "But I need you to try to keep them alive." He paused and looked at us both, then focused hard on Jerome. "Do this one for me."

Jerome Freeman sighed heavily, like the resignation came from the very bottom of his barrel of a chest. "We will do our best," he promised. He took the bottle of whiskey and refilled all three glasses, then drank his down in a couple of swallows. He turned to me and said, "Young Jake, let's have a look at your gear and mebbe get you some target practice while's I think over how we're gonna ketch these two fellas."

He led me outside and untied the black warhorse from the hitching post in front of the jail. The animal looked like it was bred to pull a giant plow, with hooves as big as buckets. He was at least sixteen hands tall and looked majestic enough for a king to ride. Jerome caught me staring at his mount and he chuckled.

"Big fella like me needs a big horse," he said. "This here's a Percheron. Knights in old England used to use 'em when they fought each other with those long spear-things because they can carry the metal armor they wore back then."

I nodded. "I've never seen such a big horse."

Jerome patted the animal's neck. "Ol' Stanley here's been a good horse to me. I know you got a good mount, yourself." He nodded across the street to where the horse I took from Callahan was still tied to a post. "What's his name?"

"I don't know," I said. "The fella that had him before me didn't say."

Jerome laughed. "Then I guess you hafta give him a new name. Looks like a George to me."

"George?" I said as he started across the street. "Shouldn't horses be named Lightning or Smoke or something like that? Not people names."

Stanley's hooves were extremely loud clops as he followed us across the packed dirt of the road. Jerome just shrugged. "He's your horse. You name him what you want. But he sure looks like a George to me."

I untied George (because that's what I ended up naming the damn horse) and we mounted up. Jerome set a course that led us out of town to the south and I didn't question him. I just rode and thought about my changing circumstances.

6

Six-Gun Practice

About a mile out of town, Jerome Freeman left the road and we galloped across a grassy meadow toward a stand of trees. When we were about fifty yards from the trees, he stopped and slid off his saddle. He took a Spencer rifle from his saddle sheath, along with his saddlebags, and motioned for me to get the Winchester off my saddle.

"Let's see how you does with a long gun first," he said. "Let George and Stanley eat up summa this sweet green grass."

"I'm not naming my horse George," I insisted.

He only chuckled again and waved his gun toward the tree line. "See can you put a bullet in that birch between the two pines," he said.

I studied the tree he'd indicated. It's true that I wasn't any great shakes with a pistol at that moment, but I had learned to be a good shot with my father's squirrel gun. Of course, the Winchester I'd recently inherited was something different than what my father had. I unsheathed my rifle and slid to the ground. The horses drifted away, munching as they walked.

"That birch?" I asked.

"Need to move closer?" Jerome asked.

"I've never actually fired this rifle," I admitted as I raised the stock to my shoulder. The sites were nice and sharp and there was just a tiny breeze blowing left to right. I aimed carefully, inhaled, and squeezed the trigger.

I splinter of bark flew off the left side of the trunk. George snorted but kept eating.

"Not bad," Jerome admitted. "Not in the center, though." In one swift, fluid motion, he lifted his Spencer to his shoulder and fired immediately. The bullet hit dead center in the trunk of the birch.

"That's good," I told him. I raised my rifle again, tried not to take as long to aim as I did last time, and fired. My shot wasn't as centered as Jerome's had been, but it was solidly in the trunk this time.

"You got the aim, but you gotta be faster," Jerome said. "Ifen that tree was shootin' back atcha, you wouldn't have time for all that aimin'."

Without saying anything, I brought the stock back to my shoulder and fired as rapidly as I could work the lever. I hit the tree with nine of the remaining twelve shots. I was secretly impressed, but tried to let on that I'd expected to do better. "Guess I wasted a couple of bullets," I said.

"Uh-huh," Jerome agreed, grinning, but rubbing his chin as if to hide it. "I think we're done with the rifle. Reload that Yallaboy and put it away."

I did as he instructed while he replaced the spent cartridge from his own rifle and put it back in the saddle sheath.

"Now what?" I asked.

"Let's cut this distance in half and see what you can do with that shiny new pistol," he answered. "It's as shiny black and just as pretty as the first woman I bedded," Jerome added when I drew the pistol as we walked, flashing all of his big white teeth at me in a grin.

I looked away and didn't say anything. I sure didn't want to talk about women. He seemed to sense he'd triggered something in me, and he let it go without saying more. We reached what he felt was a good spot and he stopped walking.

"You ever had any trainin' with a pistol?" he asked me.

"No."

"Well, you just gotta imagine that it's a part of your hand," he said thoughtfully. "The barrel is a long finger. You point it at what you want, then pulled the trigger." He looked at the birch, then back at me. "You just draw and shoot six at that ol' tree and we'll see what you do."

I missed the first two completely, grazed the right side of the trunk with my third, missed again, used the sights to actually aim with the fifth shot, and scored a good hit, but felt guilty for using the sights and didn't do it for the sixth and missed again. Jerome grunted, took off his big black hat and rubbed the palm of his hand over his short-cropped curly hair before putting the hat back on.

"You gonna need some practice," he said.

"How many times can you hit it?" I asked. It sounded more like a challenge than I meant it to be. I was just honestly curious about how good he was.

Jerome didn't answer with words. He'd been facing me, but he turned toward the tree, his hand a dark blur as his Colt cleared leather. There were six sharp cracks, one after another, and each one sent bits of wood flying off the trunk of the birch tree.

"Damn," I said, and I knew my mouth was hanging open. I knew then I was in the presence of someone who could be very dangerous. "You shoot like an outlaw," I told him.

Jerome was reloading his gun. He lifted his eyes to look at me without raising his head. "I shoots like a man that wants to stay alive," he said. "Reload and try again."

After emptying two more cylinders with basically the same results, I was feeling pretty discouraged. "It doesn't feel the same as when I was fighting those two men," I complained.

"Of course not," Jerome said. "Your fight-or-flight instincts was kicked in. You had to focus more 'cause they was shootin' back atcha. That birch ain't throwed so much as a acorn your way. You don't feel threatened."

I started to remind him that birch trees didn't produce acorns, but let that go. I got his meaning. "So, what do I do?"

"Keep practicin'," he said. "You gotta practice 'til that gun feels like a part of your hand. Reload, holster it, and draw and fire again. One shot, then back in the holster, then do it again."

So it went until late afternoon. I used up all the cartridges in my belt, but Jerome had more in his saddle bags. He said I could pay him back from my reward money. I loaded, drew, and fired that pistol for hours. I did get better, but I never did get six shots from one cylinder into that poor old tree. I have to wonder if that thing lived after that day. We sure put a lot of lead in it.

On the way back into town I asked what hotel we were going to stay at and Jerome gave me a sideways stare. "You still ain't ketchin' on, young Jake. I'll be lucky if they let me bed down in the livery stable with the horses. But you go on and get you a nice hotel with a real soft bed."

I got his meaning and felt stupid for not realizing the problem before I spoke. "Sorry," I said. "I guess we'll both be in the livery stable."

"Ain't no sense in you sleeping in the hay. Go on and get you a hotel room," Jerome said.

"If we're going to be partners, we do things together," I told him.

He grinned and nodded. "We'll get supplies and head out in the morning," he said.

"Do we have a plan yet?" I asked.

"Oh, I gots a plan. You'll like it, young Jake."

I wasn't sure I liked being called "young Jake" and I sure didn't like that he wasn't telling me what was on his mind, but Jerome Freeman was a hard man to argue with.

7

BEGINNER'S LUCK ENDS

At sunup, we were saddling our horses, then led them out of the livery stable, still brushing hay off our clothes. Stanley's giant feet drowned out George's almost dainty-sounding clopping as we walked.

"We'll tie up at the store, then see about some breakfast," Jerome said.

The store wasn't open yet, but we tied our horses to the rail in front and started for the restaurant on down the street. I could see men going in and, as we got closer, I saw through a big glass window men and women seated inside. "How are we going in there?" I asked.

"You go on in and have a seat," Jerome said. "They'll serve me around back."

"I told you, we're partners," I reminded. "I guess we'll both be eating in the back."

We were served plates of biscuits and gravy with scrambled eggs and bacon, but the man who served the food did it with a nasty glare that seemed to be directed mostly at me.

"What's his problem?" I asked.

Jerome gave off the deep chuckle again. "They don't think much of a white man who'd rather eat with a black man."

"Do you think that'll ever change?" I asked him.

Jerome shrugged and shoveled food into his face. The spoon looked like something from a little girl's play set in his massive fist. "Not whilest I'm alive, I reckon," he said.

The storekeeper did allow him inside, but made sure he waited on every other white customer before getting around to us. Jerome ordered coffee, beans, flower, beef jerky, a bag of hard candy, and one hundred rounds of ammunition for our pistols. The storekeeper, an older man with a nearly bald head and half-spectacles on the tip of his nose, pursed his lips at the ammunition order. I waited to see if he'd say something, but he didn't. As the man was bundling our supplies, Sheriff Brad Harrison entered the store and greeted Jerome, then me.

"I saw your mounts over here," he said. "Come on over to the office when you're done and I'll give you the papers you need to bring in Dewey and Buckles and anyone else riding with them."

"We'll be there," Jerome promised. Then he turned to the storekeeper and grinned that huge, dazzling grin. "We's about done here?"

The storekeeper pushed the bundled merchandise across the counter without saying anything. Jerome handed him some money and turned his back on the store. I followed him outside, where he pulled two boxes of cartridges from a bundle and tossed them to me.

"Put one in your bag and reload that belt whilest we're at the sheriff's office," he said. "You carry summa this other stuff, too. George can handle it."

"His name isn't George," I said as I took half the provisions and put them in my own saddlebags.

"Yessuh, boss," Jerome answered. "Whatever you say, boss."

"I think I know why you keep getting shot in the ass," I said as we crossed the street.

Jerome laughed and opened the door to the sheriff's office.

The lawman was sitting at his desk with a white ceramic mug of coffee steaming in front of him. He stood up and welcomed the newcomers, pouring us each a cup of coffee and motioning us to the chairs. "You ready to head out?" he asked.

"We're ready," Jerome answered.

"What about you, Jacob?" the sheriff asked. "Ready for your first job?"

"I think so," I said.

"Nervous?"

"Maybe a little," I admitted. "I've never gone hunting men before. And I have this partner who has a plan he won't tell me about." I'd taken off my gun belt before sitting down and now opened a box of bullets to start refilling it.

Sheriff Brad Harrison chuckled. He looked to Jerome and asked, "So, what is it?"

"I figger to send young Jake here on ahead of me," Jerome said. "I figger they'll try to do him just like the other two did, with one of 'em comin' up on him and bein' all friendly, while the other acts like the bad man."

"That's not how it was," I argued, a bullet poised over a loop in the belt. Jerome held up his finger to cut me off.

"I guarantee you that was the plan, but you smelled it out," he said. "Now, these men won't know how it ended for their partners on the other side of town, so we'll just do the same thing, but when that second man comes ridin' up on you, I'll be doin' the same."

"Are you okay with that?" the sheriff asked me.

"What if they just shoot me?" I asked Jerome.

"Brad here says they ain't been shootin' no one. Just robbin' 'em. Maybe roughin' 'em up a little," he said.

I didn't like it, but I shrugged. "I guess it might work."

"Just remember we want them alive if at all possible," Sheriff Harrison said.

"We know that," Jerome said. He blew over the top of his coffee and took a sip, then put the cup down and turned to me. "Jake, you best go on. Don't look back for me. I gots me a spyglass and I'll be watchin'. Don't you worry none."

I had the belt loaded by this time. I looked up from checking that my pistol was loaded. "You're not even riding out of town with me?" I asked.

"Nah. It's best if we ain't seen leavin' together," Jerome said. "I'll be leaving right after you, but I'm goin' a different way to circle around. You'll be okay."

"Said the fisherman to the worm," I mumbled. The other men laughed at me. I took a couple quick sips of the hot black coffee, then stood up, belted on my gun, and made for the door. "I guess I'll be see you up the trail then." It was something I'd heard one cowboy say to another back in San Antonio. The other men snickered.

"Be careful," the sheriff said as I closed the door.

I untied and mounted my horse and headed him west along the main street. The town was coming to life, with wagons rolling up the street, pairs of women walking the boardwalk looking into shop windows, and there was the hammering of a blacksmith somewhere nearby. I gave George a touch with my spurs and he sped up to a canter. Soon, the town faded to a cabin here and there, and then we were back in open country.

"He's nuts if he thinks I'm naming you George, like the old king of England," I said to my horse's ears.

We weren't more than a couple of miles out of town when I saw two riders coming from the west. I didn't think a lot of it because it didn't fit into the plan Jerome had laid out. I saw that one was a man in his mid-thirties and the other one was younger. Instead of moving to one side of the rode, they split up so that one would pass on either side of me. If I'd had more experience, I would have recognized that was a real bad sign.

"That's Callahan's horse alright," the older man said. "This the fella you saw ride it into town?"

"That's him, alright," the younger man said, nodding and looking back to the older man.

That's when I recognized Albert Dewey's scarred cheek and black eyes. I grabbed for my Colt, but he was so much faster and there I was, sitting on a dead man's horse, staring into the black barrel of a Colt revolver pointed right between my eyes.

"What's your name, boy?" Dewey asked me.

"Jacob Wolf," I answered, trying as hard as I could to keep my voice steady.

"Was anybody with him in town?" Dewey asked his companion.

"No, but that sheriff took him out of the saloon," the other man said. "That's when I saw John and Simon draped over horses in the street. I heard some black bounty hunter brought 'em in."

I remembered the two men who'd looked directly at me when Sheriff Harrison asked who'd ridden the black stallion with the white sock and blaze on its face to the saloon. This man was one of those two. Dewey was not the man he'd been with, obviously, and now I began to worry about how many men were in this gang. The unwavering gun pointed at my face reminded me that probably wasn't going to be my concern for too much longer.

"Did you kill Kepford and Callahan?" Dewey asked me.

"I did," I answered. "They tried to rob me."

"You look like a tenderfoot playing gunfighter to me, boy," Dewey said. "How'd you kill both of them? Kepford was almost as fast as me."

I swallowed. "Beginner's luck, I guess."

Dewey actually allowed the tiniest of grins, but it disappeared instantly. "Why didn't you bring them in?"

"I didn't know they were wanted. They just tried to rob me, so I shot them," I said.

"What about the bounty hunter?" he asked.

I lied and hoped he'd believe me. "He's getting the money. I got to keep the horse."

"You are green," Dewey said. "Those two both had prices on their heads. About six hundred dollars, last I heard."

I didn't correct him.

"You sure you don't have some of that money?" he asked.

"I can check him," the younger man offered.

"We'll check him," Dewey said. "Jacob Wolf, I want you to hand over that pistol real slow. Kind of like your life depends on it."

There was nothing else to do. Dying without firing a shot was not the story I wanted told back in San Antonio, and there just was no possibility I was going to be able to shoot either of these men with that Colt aimed between my eyes. I wondered where Jerome was and pictured him still sitting in the sheriff's office, finishing that mug of coffee. I eased my pistol from its shiny black holster and handed it over. Dewey took it and lowered his own weapon, but kept it in his hand, putting mine into his holster.

"Let's take him to see the boys," Dewey said, then motioned for me to ride ahead of him and his partner.

8

A PERSONAL POSSESSION

Of course I thought about running, just digging my spurs into the horse and letting him fly. He was a good horse, but I knew he couldn't outrun a bullet. I thought about wheeling him around and charging back at the two men, but figured I'd be dead before George got himself turned around.

I thought a lot about Jerome Freeman and his spyglass he'd said he had. Was he watching us? Had he seen me get captured and gone ahead to set an ambush? Was he going to use that Spencer rifle to shoot these two from the trees? The more we rode, the less likely any of that seemed to be.

And finally, I thought of my death. It would be remarked with nothing more than a tiny news article. Something like, *Jacob Wolf, drifter, was the latest victim killed by Albert Dewey's gang of ruffians. Wolf was unarmed and died without a fight.* If such a thing even made the papers back in San Antonio, I imagined Rebecca Dickenson reading it and shaking her head and telling her pa, "I knew he'd never amount to anything."

"See that clump of scrub oak over to your left, boy?" Dewey called from behind me. "Angle over there toward those."

I did what he told me to do, and as I got closer I saw that the trees were on the edge of a sharp slope that led down into a dusty little valley where a lone house no bigger than a shack sat beside a weather-beaten barn and a split-rail corral. There was a thin line of smoke coming from the cabin and two horses milled around the corral. If there were two horses, I figured there were two more men down there, and that made the odds even worse for me.

"Watch your footing, boy," Dewey called. "I'd hate for you to fall off that stolen horse and break your neck too soon." His partner laughed at that.

There was a bit of a path leading down, but it was steep and required all my attention to navigate it. I gave George his head, pretty much, and he picked his way down. I was scared there'd be a rattler in the tall grass and it would send us all tumbling down the hill, George rolling over me and killing me that way. But all of us made it to the bottom without incident. When I looked up, two men were standing on the sagging porch of the cabin to watch us.

I waited for the crack of Jerome's Spencer from the top of the hill, but it never came. We rode up to the house and Dewey told me to dismount. My fingers brushed the stock of the Winchester, and I considered it, but there was no chance of using that. Dewey told his partner to take the horses to the corral and make sure they were fed.

"Hurry up, though," he said. "The trial'll be starting soon and you'll be wanted on the jury."

The man laughed, then said, "I vote we execute him."

"We'll hear his story first. Then we'll execute him," Dewey said. All four of the outlaws laughed at that one. "Go on in the house, Jacob Wolf," he told me. The two men on the porch stepped aside so I could pass through the door.

The interior of the cabin was a bleak as the exterior. There was a table with one chair, a milk stool, and an upside down bucket. The fireplace was small but there was a pot bubbling over the fire. The lone cot had a blanket on it and there were three other bedrolls in various stages of disarray around the edges of the single room. Under the smell of cooking beans I could detect mouse turds.

"Alright, boy, how about you hand over that reward money now," Dewey said.

I turned to face him. David Buckles was to his right and the other man to his left. "I don't have it," I said. "I told you that. All I got was the horse."

Albert Dewey sighed. "Les, tie his hands behind him."

"No, I don't think so," I said. In that moment, I went cold. It was just like back on the trail when I saw Callahan riding up behind me and Kepford and I knew what was happening. I didn't have a gun, though. I stepped forward, my fists clenched at my sides. If this was how I died, so be it. I'd be damned if I'd be trussed up like a hog going to slaughter. "Kill me now if that's what you want to do. Search my dead body like the jackals you are, you dirty son—"

Yeah, that's as far as I got. I was so focused on Albert Dewey and the pistol he was pointing at me that I didn't notice David Buckles stepping up. Later on, I realized he carried his pistol on his left side, but I'd already figured out he was a southpaw by that time. I saw his fist an instant before it smashed into my cheek. I staggered sideways and before I could turn to face him, he caught me in the jaw with a haymaker — again from his left — and I never even saw the floor coming up to greet me.

I had a vague sense of being jostled around, and when I was able to clear my head I found myself sitting up with my wrists tied tightly behind my back. The pockets of my trousers were turned out and my shirt was untucked, so I guessed they'd gone ahead and searched me for the money. I licked my lips, which felt funny, and tasted blood. I pulled my knees up and rested my forehead on them, looking down, and there was no fresh blood dripping off my face, so I thought that was good, but guessed Buckles must have busted at least part of my lip with that first punch.

"You already been beatin' on 'im," somebody said. I looked up to see that Dewey's companion from the trail had returned. He gawked at me like I was a sideshow attraction.

"He got brave for a second there," Dewey said. He sat in the only chair, my holster on the table in front of him and my pistol in his hand. "This here belt is still stiff and there's hardly a scratch to show that you've drawed this pistol," he said to me.

"Kepford commented on that, too, before I killed him," I said.

He shook his head and holstered my gun, pushing the rig away from him. "I still don't know how you did that. He was fast and a straight shot. Callahan wasn't much, but Kepford ... Mean son-of-a-bitch, too."

"I left them both for the coyotes and buzzards," I said.

"Um-hmm. But then a black bounty hunter found them. That's a strange coincidence. You working with that bounty hunter?" he asked me again.

"I never saw him before the sheriff took me to his office." That was the truth.

"Ol' Brad Harrison," Dewey said with a grin. "He used to be a helluva man. Now he's all bound up with the law and jurisdiction."

Dewey's friends all laughed about that.

"You said we were gonna try him, Albert," the man from the trail said. "You gonna be the judge?"

"I am," he said. "You checked his saddlebags?"

"Nothin' but food and bullets. No money," the man said.

"Well, I guessed that," Dewey said. "He had two dollars and fifty-three cents in his pockets." He looked directly at me. "And a letter from a girl named Rebecca."

My face burned with anger and I glared back at him. How dare he take my letter. Did he read it? Could he read? He must have if he knew her name.

"Our defendant here got the ol' heave-ho from the lady love he followed west from Kentucky," Dewey said. "She appreciated his companionship, but she didn't know what love was then. She found it, though, with some fella named Parker, and she insists Jacob Wolf stop trying to see her." He grinned as he finished his summary of my most personal possession. His friends all had another good laugh at my expense.

"I'll kill you," I said, my voice low and feral. I felt like a trapped wolf right at that moment. I wanted that man's blood more than I'd ever wanted anything before. Except Rebecca. "If I have to come back from the grave, I'll kill you for this."

"I've never been one to get scared of boogeymen," Dewey said. He pulled my pistol from its holster again and banged the butt down on the table. "Let's get this trail going so we can eat after we deliver justice." The other three men whooped, but then Buckles held out a hand.

"Hold on a minute," he said. "I need to go to the shitter again."

Dewey gave him an exasperated look, but the other man who'd been in the cabin sniggered and said, "He ate some persimmons that ain't wantin' to stay inside a' him." Buckles gave him an obscene gesture, but was already nearly running out of the cabin.

9

Spencer Talks

The cabin was pretty quiet in Buckles' absence. I was still seething over Dewey reading that final letter from Rebecca. He seemed to just be irritated over the delay, while the other two men sat by the fireplace and passed a bottle of whiskey between them. I tried to reach my chin down to my unbuttoned shirt pocket to see if I could feel the missing letter. Dewey noticed me.

"I put it back in there," he said. "You can die with her final words on you."

I sat still and refused to look at him, but was grateful for that, at least.

"Dammit!" Dewey finally exploded. "Les, get out there and see if he fell in the damn hole."

The one who'd ridden in with us scrambled up from the floor and crammed his hat onto his head as he fled through the door. He wasn't gone more than a couple of minutes when I got my first whiff of smoke. Not from the fireplace, from closer to me. Then I saw it come streaming through cracks in the plank floor in gray clouds. I rolled away just as orange tongues of flame licked up through the floor.

Dewey and the other man jumped to their feet and the idiot with the whiskey dropped the bottle, which sent flammable alcohol racing toward the flames. They both ran for the door. Dewey was smart enough to draw his gun before he ran out, but it didn't matter. He was still in the doorway when I heard the crack of a rifle. Dewey's pistol and a spray of blood flew back into the cabin as I rolled away from the whiskey that made a *whoosh* sound as it caught fire.

"You there, throw down your gun, then you two git back in there and drag that other man outta there so I can see who all I got." I knew that voice, and, despite some serious concerns over the way the fire was spreading, figured out that Jerome was pretending he didn't know me.

"I ain't goin' back in there!" the man I didn't have a name for yelled back.

"Then you gonna die where you stand," Jerome called.

Dewey and his companion came back in. If looks were knives, Dewey would have scalped me with the way he was glaring at me. His hand was bleeding where Jerome had shot off two fingers. The two men came through the smoke and fire and hauled me to my feet. "Are you working with him?" Dewey growling into my ear.

"Who?" I asked. "Is it the sheriff?"

Dewey shoved me toward the door so hard that I stumbled and couldn't navigate the single step from the porch to the ground. I managed to turn my head so I didn't land on my face, but it was still a pretty hard hit. Then the shooting started.

Two shots from a pistol came from inside the cabin. Jerome fired once from his Spencer. The man who wasn't Dewey doubled over in the doorway and dropped my gun onto the porch as he fell. Another shot from inside sent a puff of dirt up to Jerome's right. He raised the rifle and shot again. There was a cry of agony inside the cabin.

"For the love of Pete," Jerome said, and I think he meant it as a curse. He raced by me, jumped over the dead man in the doorway and disappeared into the smoke. He came out a moment later dragging

Dewey by an arm and carrying my gun belt. He kicked the dead man out of his way, then kicked my pistol toward me before flinging Dewey down beside me. Albert Dewey took a step, screamed, and collapsed. I saw that his right knee seemed to be shattered because his lower leg was at an odd angle.

"You alright, young Jake?" Jerome asked as he bent over and sliced through the ropes holding me with a knife he kept at his side.

"I'm fine," I answered. "But I'm going to kill that man."

"Nah, I can't let ya do that," Jerome said. "Did he rough ya up some?"

"He ..." I trailed off, unwilling to describe what Buckles had done.

Dewey, though, had no problem with it. "I read his letter from a girl that used him and threw him away for being nothin' but Tennessee trash," he said. "I shoulda known you were working with him," he snarled at me.

Jerome let me kick him once in the head before pulling me away. He was a fair man that way. Behind us, the back wall of the cabin caved in, which brought down the roof. We were pushed forward in a wave of heat.

"Where are Buckles and the other one?" I asked, glancing around.

"They's in the outhouse," Jerome said, motioning to the little wooden building between the house and barn. There was banging come from inside it, but what I really noticed was that there was a lasso around the building and the other end of the rope was tied to Stanley's saddle horn while the giant horse stood patiently at the end of the taut rope, keeping the door of the outhouse firmly closed.

"I'll be damned," I said, and laughed.

"Pick up your gun, young Jake, and keep an eye on our friend here whilest I go deal with those two," Jerome said.

I did as he told me, but really, at that point, between being shot twice and kicked in the head once, Dewey wasn't much of a threat, so I got to watch Jerome stand in front of the outhouse with his rifle trained on the door while he called his horse to him. Stanley tossed his head and ambled close, letting slack into the rope. The shitter door burst open and the two men tumbled out. They looked up from the ground to find the rifle trained on them. I couldn't help but notice they both had large bumps and trickles of blood on their heads. Jerome got them onto their feet and led them and Stanley over to us.

"Jacob, can you keep all three of these fellas covered for a minute?" he asked.

"I reckon so," I answered.

Jerome pulled two sets of wrist shackles from a saddlebag and put one on each of the two men still on their feet. He looked down at Dewey and said, "I guess we hafta tend to his wounds before we lock him up."

Just then I smelled something, and Jerome seemed to smell it, too. It was the smell of burning meat. Jerome took off at a run, back toward the collapsed cabin. He disappeared into a cloud of black smoke, but came back a moment later, dragging the body of the dead man. He got the smoking body away from the house and rolled it around in the dirt until he was sure there was no fire, then came back over to us.

"What's his name?" Jerome asked.

Buckles and Les were silent.

"Well, I guess we don't have to take the whole body back to town to collect the ree-ward," Jerome said. "I'll just cut off his head and take that. Easier to carry thattaway."

"You ain't cuttin' off no white man's head," Buckles spat.

"Then you tell me his name and I might just let y'all bury him," Jerome said, grinning at the two smaller men.

"Name's Tom Blevins," Les said.

"That's right reasonable of ya," Jerome said. "Who are you?"

"Les McCarty."

"I'm glad you're more agreeable than your friend Mr. Buckles here," Jerome said.

"Listen, man, I ain't done nothin' real bad," Les said. "Just stealin'. Albert and John and David here did all the killin'. Can't you just let me go?"

Jerome turned to me and fixed me with his dark brown eyes. "Young Jake, this here happens right often," he said. "What do you do in a situation like this? We gots no papers with the name Les McCarty on 'em."

"We got papers saying we can bring in everyone riding with Dewey and Buckles," I answered.

"But Mr. McCarty here has been right helpful and he promises he ain't kilt nobody. Ain't that right?" Jerome turned to Les as he asked.

"Yessir, that's right. I ain't killed nobody," he gushed.

"Obviously he wouldn't lie about that," I said, playing along. I shrugged. "But, we're supposed to bring in everybody. I guess the sheriff or the courts will let him go if they think he should be free."

"Wooooo-eeeee!" Jerome whooped. He pointed a finger as big as a .44 Colt barrel at me. "I knowed you'd make the right decision, young Jake. I just knowed I could count on you." I wasn't sure how to respond, so I just shook my head and proceeded to reload the spent chambers of my pistol. Jerome asked, "You got any doctorin' skills?"

"Nope," I answered.

"Well then, how about you oversee these two in carryin' Tom Blevins into the barn while I take a look at the wounds on their friend," he suggested. "I figure I'll have to splint that leg and wrap up his hand.

Them fingers musta cooked in the house. We might just sleep here tonight and head back to town in the morning."

10

REMEMBERING HOME

We slept in the barn that night. Jerome bound up Albert Dewey's shattered leg with four pieces of stove wood and some rope and poured whiskey on the stumps of his missing fingers, but Dewey was in and out of consciousness all night, moaning with a fever. The other two men were bound at the wrists, with another set of shackles holding them together but separated by the slats of a low wall dividing two horse stalls. They complained about that until Jerome offered to sing them to sleep with the butt of his revolver.

Jerome and I took turns keeping watch during the night. Outside, in the dark, the burned-down house was a blacker shape against the ground, sometimes with orange eyes opening here and there, like a monster from a kids' story. I was surprised nobody had come to investigate the smoke or fire. As we were getting ready to bed down, I asked Jerome if he thought one of these outlaws owned the land. He chuckled.

"Naw, young Jake. They's lots of places like this all over Texas," he said. "Folks that owned this prolly couldn't make a go of it and just lef' it. That happens a lot. They just move on. Prolly owe some bank money. These rascals just found it and used it."

"So, you don't think they killed the people who were here?" I asked.

Jerome looked around in the evening light, rubbed his chin, then said, "No, I reckon not. Place hasn't been farmed in a while. I s'pect it was empty when they got here. You're sure free to ask 'em." He grinned at me.

"They'd just lie about it," I said.

"Like as not," Jerome agreed.

I sat up in the early morning hours, my pistol held loosely in my hand dangling off my pulled-up knees and recounted how I'd had to tell the story about being captured without even a fight. Jerome didn't say I should have done this or that, like I thought he might.

"Dewey was going into town, huh?" he mused. "Ol' Sheriff Brad Harrison woulda liked that. I wonder how that woulda gone."

I felt a good deal of shame over my effortless capture, passive captivity, and non-participation in my own rescue. Nothing was really going the way it was supposed to. I wondered again what the papers would have said if I had put up a fight and been gunned down. I was sure I wouldn't have gotten more than a mention. Unless I'd managed to kill Dewey before I died. At the time of my capture, that hadn't seemed likely enough to even give it a try.

My thoughts drifted back to Rebecca, with her long brown curls and brown eyes that were like dollops of honey when the sun shone onto her face. I remember sitting with her under an oak tree back in Kentucky or along the trail to Texas after a day of travel and just watching her mouth as she talked to me about stuff that didn't even matter. She'd catch me at it and get embarrassed and tell me I was awful, but her blush seemed to say something else. At least, I'd thought so at the time.

Maybe she'd just been feeling shame over the fact she was leading me on a road to heartbreak and she knew it. She knew she didn't love me, even when she said she did. I'd just been a companion. Someone to listen to her prattle. I should have given her a puppy before she left Kentucky and just stayed on my family farm.

My pa had been pretty mad about me leaving. He said he needed me. He couldn't afford to hire someone to do the work I did. "If you leave, we'll lose this farm. Are you gonna take away your ma's home?" he'd said. But Ma had come to talk to me late in the evening.

"You love her, don't you?" she asked in her soft, knowing voice.

"I do, Ma," I answered.

"I can't say she's the one I would have picked out for you," Ma said. "Rebecca reminds me of a stream running over rocks. There's a lot of babble, but no depth."

I started to protest, but Ma took my right hand between her two, small, callused hands and squeezed it. "Hush, Jacob," she said. "Mothers are often wrong about the women replacing them in their boys' hearts." We sat quietly for a few minutes. "If you love her, you have to go with her. And it's right a boy leaves home to make it on his own. You're old enough."

"What about you and Pa?" I asked. "Pa said you'll lose the farm if I leave."

Ma smiled wistfully and I remembered the evening breeze fluttering a loose lock of her blond hair so that it streamed beside her head like a battle flag. "Men can sure be dramatic sometime," she said. "We'll get along. There'll be some adjustments, but we'll get along. He'll miss you, though. I suppose he can't say that to you, but he will."

She was right. Pa didn't say he'd miss me. He didn't tell me to come back if things didn't work out. When I told him I was going, he didn't speak to me again, and didn't leave the barn to see me off, but left Ma standing alone on our back porch, waving to me and crying until I was out of sight.

I couldn't decide if I hated my pa for that, but I was sure mad at him.

Dawn finally came. I made coffee over a small fire and Jerome shared out strips of jerky for breakfast. Dewey was still moaning and thrashing around sometimes. His partners eyed him warily.

"He can't ride," Buckles said.

"It's a short ride back to town," Jerome said. "We'll put him over his saddle."

"He needs a wagon," Buckles said. "He ain't wanted dead."

"We ain't got no wagon," Jerome answered. "It'd take longer to make a travois than it's worth. We could be halfway back to town before it's made."

"Not if you let us go to help," Blevins suggested. Jerome only laughed at him.

Breakfast finished, I put out the fire and helped Jerome put Dewey across his saddle as gently as we could manage. The wounded man's skin was almost as hot as the coals of the fire I'd just put out. Jerome was worried about Dewey's thrashing, so he tied his unhurt hand to his unhurt leg below the mare's belly.

He told me to go ahead and mount up and have my pistol ready while he brought out the other two prisoners. I did, and he led the other men out of the barn, their hands still bound in front of them, but no longer to each other. We'd saddled horses for them and they mounted reluctantly, but with my pistol pointing at their faces and Jerome's prodding them in the ribs.

"Keep your pistol on this one," Jerome said, motioning to Blevins. He tied the reins of the horse Dewey was bound to around Blevins' mount's saddle horn as he kept talking to me. "Don't ever trust your prisoners, young Jake. Why, if I was to give Mistah Blevins or Mistah Buckles here half a moment, they'd whack me over the head with the iron of those shackles and we'd have us a different situation goin' on. If you was to have to do sumpin like this on your own, you'd have wanted to tie these horses together before bringin' out your prisoners."

"Are you this white boy's school teacher?" Buckles sneered.

"Now, don't make me hafta stuff a rag in your mouth," Jerome answered as he swung into his own saddle. "Young Jake, do you want lead or drag on this outfit?"

I took the lead. Jerome caught up the reins of the two unmanned horses and followed along behind Buckles and Blevins. We considered going to the end of the little valley to avoid the steep slope we'd come down because of Dewey's condition, but I suggested that would waste a lot of time for someone who'd gladly kill us if he could. Plus, if we were trying to save him, he needed a doctor soon. Jerome agreed. The slope didn't give us too much trouble, though I thought for a minute the two horses Jerome was leading might pull him off Stanley, but Jerome kept hold and we all made it to the top without problems.

People stared and pointed as we rode back into town. By the time we arrived at the sheriff's office, Brad Harrison was standing outside waiting on us with a big grin on his face.

11

TEMPTATION

A little gray-haired doctor who looked like he might have been on hand to set the bones of Moses, had he needed it, took Dewey to his office and later in the day said he'd amputated the leg, but expected a full recovery. The other two outlaws were deposited into the town jail. The sheriff paid us the rewards for Kepford and Callahan and promised to have the rest of our money the next day.

"Too bad about the other one," Harrison said as we sat in his office. "What was his name?"

"Les McCarty," I answered.

"I don't have any posters on him, so I couldn't have paid you for him," Harrison said.

"What about them horses we brung in?" Jerome asked.

"I'll check 'em for brands and see if they're stolen," Harrison said. "I haven't heard of any horse thieving. Are you wantin' to keep 'em?"

"Nah, I figgered we'd sell 'em," Jerome said.

The sheriff nodded. "I'll check on it."

We left the sheriff to his duties when a man stepped in and said Buster King over at the general store was holding a man at gunpoint for shoplifting. Jerome joked that we could go bring that fella in for fifty dollars, but the sheriff laughed us off. It was getting late by this time and I were hungry. I asked Jerome about going to the back door of the café for some supper.

"Nah, you go on inside," he said. "I'll go around back." I started to protest, but he raised one of those ham-sized hands and cut me off. "I know what yer about to say, and I 'ppreciate it. Tomorrow, after we get the rest of our money, we's headin' down to a place I know where you'll be the one ain't so welcome. So, you eat, then go over to the saloon and have a good time."

I wanted to question him, but he said he was too powerful hungry to explain any more of the ways of the world to me today and left me there in the street. I had a peaceful, if somewhat lonely meal inside the little restaurant. The beefsteak was tender and the mashed potatoes were almost as good as Ma's, but not quite. After I ate, I considered just going back to the livery stable where I knew Jerome would sleep, or maybe even getting a hotel room, but a glance at the saloon where I'd so recently been called out by the sheriff made me want to show I was free to come and go there as I pleased.

The saloon was loud, dim, and smoky. Against the far wall a fat man with thick black hair pounded an upright piano with more enthusiasm than talent. Men sat at tables and at the bar, drinking, gambling, talking. A few looked up at me when I came in, but nobody seemed particularly interested, and that suited me right down to my boot heels. I went to the bar and ordered a cold beer, then retreated to a table by the staircase leading to the second floor to drink and watch.

I wasn't more than halfway through my beer before a blonde in a green dress that showed off her shoulders and the cleavage between her breasts fluttered into the empty chair at my table, propped her small chin in her hands, and fixed her green eyes on me. "You looked like you could use some company," she said.

"Looks can be deceiving," I told her.

"Ah, that sounds like you don't want me here," she pouted.

I turned my full attention on her. "I don't," I said. I considered apologizing, maybe even explaining myself, but I didn't want to. I suddenly didn't want to be in the saloon. I didn't want to be around anybody at all. I drained my beer and got up from the table, leaving the empty mug and the surprised girl behind.

I went into the first hotel I came to and rented a room for the night. It was the first time I'd been in a bed in a long time and I was asleep almost before my empty boots hit the floor.

The next day, I met Jerome early at the livery stable. He suggested I get a shave and a bath if I wanted it while he got us supplied for a longer ride. "I picked up a couple of posters from the sheriff," he said. "We'll be going up into the Territory in a couple of days."

"I thought we were going somewhere you could have some fun with that money," I said.

"Oh, we are. Yessir, we are. We'll be there afore dinner."

I passed up the shave and bath. I was still a young man and was mighty proud of the little patches of fuzz I'd grown on my chin and upper lip. And I just couldn't see paying for a bath when I could do that for free in any river or creek we came across. Instead, I went and bought some eggs and a few strips of bacon and we cooked them on the forge in the blacksmith shop next to the livery stable. An hour after the last bite, we were out of town, headed east.

"Is this another town we're going to?" I asked.

"Naw, just a little settlement," Jerome said. "Mostly tents. Sometimes they gotta tear down and move real quick. White folks don't like it when us colored folks gather together. Makes 'em some nervous."

"So, I'm going to be the only white person there?"

"Oh no, young Jake, you ain't goin' into the camp," Jerome said, laughing. "We'll set up our camp someways off and I'll be going in alone." He grinned at me. "But I don't plan on bein' alone all night, if you take my meanin'."

We made camp near a little U shape in a stream. Jerome left me to unsaddle the horses while he went to get cleaned up. I heard him singing some old slave spiritual song while he was in the water. When he came back he was wearing a scarlet shirt with shiny black buttons and trousers as yellow as a baby chick. He'd cleaned his boots the best he could and when he came into camp he took a rag from his saddle bags and did some brushing at his big black hat. He put it on at an angle and looked at me.

"How do I look?" he asked.

I laughed, but told him, "Those ladies in camp will line up for you."

"That's what I'm a-wantin'!" he said, and slapped me on the shoulder, which almost sent me sprawling through the willow branches and into the creek myself. "Well, you'll be just fine here, young Jake. You might hear some music later, but you best stay away."

"I'll stay right here," I said. "I'll cook up some supper, then go to sleep."

"That'll be best," he said again, then he climbed onto his big Percheron and trotted away.

I heated up some beans, a little bacon, and treated myself to a whole can of juicy peaches for supper. I wasn't tired yet, so I took a piece of an old gunny sack and rubbed George down and told him again how his name wasn't George, but I hadn't had time to settle on a better name just yet. He didn't care. The grass near the stream was tall and green and he was enjoying it. Night closed in around us. Frogs sang and sometimes I heard a fish splash. An owl hooted and crickets chirped.

Off in the distance I could hear a guitar and a fiddle and the deep, husky voice of a woman. I couldn't make out the words she was singing, but whenever she stopped there was a roar from what had to be a sizeable audience. Try as I might, I couldn't get to sleep. I just lay there wondering about what Jerome was doing and comparing it to my utter failure of an attempt to enjoy myself the night before.

I finally gave up and decided I had to go see this for myself. Just a peek wouldn't hurt anything.

12

—— ◆ ——

DOUBLE-BARRELED THREAT

Finding the settlement of tents wasn't hard to do. If my ears had failed me, my nose sure would have picked out a path. Once I got away from my own camp with its little fire and smell of horse and woods and water, I was overwhelmed with the aroma of cooking meat, and it only got stronger as the music got louder. I saw the tents through the branches of cottonwood tree and saw there was a path worn through the underbrush to the settlement, but not wanting to be seen, I pushed into the brush, moving as quietly as I could and going slow.

Looking back on it, I guess I was more surprised to find the lady squatting to pee in the brush than she was to be discovered there. She turned her face up toward me and asked, "Whatchu doin' here, white boy?" without even breaking stream.

My heart was hammering in my chest. I'd never seen a woman urinating before. I didn't know what to make of this black woman just squatted there pissing while talking to me. "I ... I heard the ... music," I stammered out.

"Oh yeah? You like that?" she asked. She stood up and straightened what was the shortest skirt I'd ever seen. It didn't go even halfway down her thighs. "Excitin', ain't it?" she asked, following my gaze.

"I'm sorry, ma'am," I said. "I'll just go on back."

"Don't go yet," she said, and to my further shock, she stepped forward and put a hand on my chest. She was a slender woman with long, delicate fingers. Her lips were very red and she smiled up at me. "You ever tried the brown sugar?"

"The what?" I was young and dumb and confused.

"If your money's the right color, I don't care what color your skin is, honey," she said.

"No," I said. "No. I'm not ... I don't ..."

"Are you tellin' me you ain't saddle-broke yet?" she asked, laughing a little.

I could smell her now. Her skin. Over the smell of cooking meat there was the smell of skin and sweat and musk and I knew I'd made a big mistake coming here. "I'll just go," I said again.

Then she slid her hand low and gripped my groin. All I could think right then was how Rebecca had said she loved me. How I thought I would make a family with her. How she would be my first and only lover. And now this whore who had pissed on the ground in front of me was touching me.

"Get away!" I shouted. I pushed her toward the tents and she cried out as she stumbled and fell onto the grass.

She lay there, propped up on her hands, looking at me. She opened her mouth to say something — to curse me, I'm sure — but before she could, another figure detached itself from the shadows beside the biggest tent and stepped out into the moonlight. He was a big black man in clean work clothes. He was taller than me, but he had a big gut and thick arms. He held a long double-barreled shotgun loosely in his right hand. When he saw the woman on the ground he shifted the gun into a more ready position.

"Camilla, whatchu doin' out there?" he called.

"They's some white boy pushin' me around," she called back.

"White boy?" he said, but it was almost like he spit the words.

I considered running, but even in my agitated frame of mind, I knew he'd raise that shotgun and let loose with both barrels. I stepped out of the brush and faced the man. Even as I prepared to speak, I felt myself going cold again. I knew this was it. This was the time I would die. It wouldn't be for glory. It wouldn't be a noble death. I'd be blown to pieces by a shotgun held by a man protecting a whore I didn't even want. I was ready, though. I just didn't care.

"I heard the music," I said, and my voice was low and flat.

"So you just come up and decided to push a woman?" the man asked. The butt of the gun was between his bicep and his meaty flank, one hand on the forward stock and the other with a finger on the triggers. The hammers were not yet pulled back.

"I walked up on her. Didn't mean any harm. She touched me."

He cocked his head at me like he wasn't sure he understood me. "You don't like it when a woman touches you?" he asked.

The music had stopped. Dozens of faces were looking through the parted tent flaps at us. I didn't see Jerome in the crowd. They watched in silence, waiting.

"You ain't the first white boy I've shot," the man said.

I stared back without saying anything. I'd never shot a black man, but I didn't think that would impress him.

"Young Jake, I tol' you to stay in camp." It was Jerome's voice. He approached us slowly from my right. The buttons on his shirt were all in the wrong holes and there was a plump black woman with short hair and bare feet trying to keep up with him while holding the top of her dress over her massive breasts.

"This boy wit' you?" the man with the shotgun asked.

"He's my partner," Jerome answered. "Jake, get on outta here."

"Too late," the man said. "He leaves now, he's likely to bring more white folk."

"He ain't gonna bring nobody," Jerome argued. "Is you, Jake?"

"No." I kept my eyes on the man with the gun.

"Jacob!" Jerome snapped. "This ain't no man you wanna mess with. And he's got the drop on you. You ain't gotta chance."

"It doesn't matter," I said, and in that moment I meant it. I was tired of it. Tired of hurting. Tired of feeling nothing but pain and hate every time I saw a woman. Tired of knowing they were all like her.

"Young Jake, I'm tellin' ya —" Jerome never got to finish that sentence.

The man with the shotgun moved his right thumb to pull back the hammers of his weapon. For me, at that time, it seemed his thumb moved in slow motion and I knew as sure as I knew the sun would rise in the morning whether I was there to see it or not, that he was going to pull those triggers as soon as the gun was cocked. His lips were curled in a snarl and his eyes were fixed on me as those twin barrels rose a little higher.

Jerome had taught me well about the smooth motion of drawing my pistol. I swept it up from my hip, cocking it as my arm moved, and pointed it where I wanted the bullet to go into the man's chest, then squeezed the trigger. My gun cracked. The other man jerked, stepped backward, his shotgun pointing toward the moon before I saw the flash and heard the thunder of both barrels going off. The recoil sent the gun slamming backward out of his grasp so that it hit the ground before he did. The man twitched a few times. A bubble of blood formed in his open mouth and popped, then he was still.

The whore — Camilla — dropped down beside the dead pimp and began to cry onto his chest in loud, dramatic wails.

"Dammit." It was Jerome. "Get my boots, woman," he said.

A man with a fiddle and bow in his right hand stepped out of the tent. He was wearing a flannel suit and had fuzzy gray hair and a stooped back. He looked at the dead man and looked at me, my pistol still in my hand, but down at my side. He looked at Jerome. "He's with you?"

"Yeah," Jerome said, and I heard the embarrassment in his voice.

"Get him outta here," the man said. "You, too. Get out. You ain't welcome here no more."

The woman he'd been with hurried back with Jerome's boots. He struggled to pull them on while standing upright, but he did it. Someone else led Stanley out from inside the gathering of tents and handed the reins over to Jerome. He mounted the massive horse and brought him over to me.

"You ridin' or walkin'?"

I turned away from him and walked out on the path beaten through the grass and brush, the giant horse clomping along behind me.

13

CARDS ON THE TABLE

Jerome didn't speak to me until he'd unsaddled Stanley, laid out his bedroll, then sat down on a rock and stirred the fire back to life. I figured he was going to ask me why I'd gone to the settlement, or get mad because I'd spoiled his fun. I was wrong.

"Who are you, Jacob Wolf?" he asked. The dumb country accent was almost completely gone from his voice. He poked at some burning branches in the campfire with his stick, then looked up at me and repeated his question. "Who are you?"

"I told you my name," I said sullenly. The coldness had left me. I was angry and tired and really just wanted to be left alone.

"Jacob Wolf from a farm in Kentucky," Jerome said. "You went to San Antonio, Texas, and worked in a hardware store but didn't like it, so you bought a gun and left. But there's more to it."

"Why are you talking different?" I demanded.

"People expect certain things, Jacob, and they feel better when they get what they expect," he said. "My size is intimidating enough, so I have to play the dumb nigger around white people to ease their minds."

"Can you read?"

"No, I can't read," he admitted. "You can't really learn to read just by watching and listening to others, but you can learn to speak. Now, tell me who you are."

"Why do you care?"

"Because if we're going to ride together, work together, and depend on each other for our lives, I need to know who I have as a partner," he said. "I saw something in your eyes tonight that I don't like. Not at all."

"What?" I ask him.

"I saw a man who wants to die," he said.

I couldn't answer him.

"Why?" he asked.

"What do you mean?" I asked in return. "How could you know that?"

He sighed and poked at the fire some more. "I've been doing this job for a long time," he said. "I have to catch men who have been kept in cages. They'd rather die than go back to that life. They've done things to make me shoot them. Kill them. They used me to kill themselves instead of going back to jail. You had that look when you was facing down Toby."

I didn't respond.

"Why?" he asked me again.

I didn't want to answer. I didn't want to share my stupid sad story. But this man had saved my life. He'd taken time to train me. He'd just revealed a huge secret about himself. I owed him. "She just used me," I said. I didn't mean for it to come out as a whisper, but that was all I could muster. I tried again. "She used me. She said she loved me. Made me think we'd get married in San Antonio. But once we got there, I wasn't good enough. She said she could never marry a clerk in her father's store or the son of a poor Kentucky farmer. There was the son of a rancher ..."

"A woman," Jerome said. He shook his big head. "I should have known. Dewey said something about a woman."

"He took the letter she wrote me telling me to stop coming around trying to court her," I admitted. "He gave it back, but he read it to those other men." I unbuttoned my shirt pocket and took out the folded square of paper. Jerome didn't ask me to, but I unfolded it and read it to him

Jacob, I can never thank you enough for your friendship back there in Kentucky and for your companionship as we travelled to San Antonio. It was delightful of you to listen to me talk and I often found you to be amusing and charming. I apologize if my friendship led you to believe there was something more between us, however, we would never be a suitable match. I am sorry to be blunt, but your insistence in calling on me makes it necessary: It simply is not fitting for a girl of my position to marry a man of your lower position. Parker Davenport has asked my father for permission to court me and Father has given it. I do not want to see you come to harm, so please, I implore you to keep your distance and give up this silly idea you have about us getting married. Sincerely Yours, Rebecca Dickenson.

I folded the letter again and put it back in my pocket.

"So, why are you trying to get yourself killed?" he asked me again.

"It's dumb," I said, and I knew in saying it that I sounded like a child.

"We're puttin' it all on the table tonight," he said. "I want to know."

I sighed and looked up at the sky full of glittering stars and wished I could just pop out of my body and go up up up to those stars and away from all the questions and sadness and pain. But I couldn't. "I thought if I died a good death, like in the stories, word would get back to her and she'd feel bad for what she did to me."

Jerome stared at me for a long while, as if he had a hard time comprehending what I'd told him. "Toby spreading your guts across half the state of Texas with that shotgun would have been a good death?" he asked.

I shook my head. "It was just when she touched me, that woman, it brought back all the broken promises and I felt so bad I ... I just wanted to end it."

Jerome was quiet for a few minutes more, then he flipped his stick into the fire and stood up. He unbuttoned his misbuttoned shirt and shrugged out of it, then unbuttoned the top of his stained white long johns and pulled his arms out, letting the top of the garment hang down past his knees. He turned his broad back to me. "Look at this," he ordered.

His back was crisscrossed with old scars. There was hardly an inch of undamaged flesh to be seen from the waist of his bright yellow pants to his thick neck. The scars glistened shiny orange in the flickering firelight.

"You see that?" he demanded.

"Yes," I said quietly.

He turned back to me and pulled on his underwear, leaving it unbuttoned down his chest. He sat down and glared at me. "I was born a slave," he said. "You probably guessed that. I was always bigger and stronger than the other boys, so I was supposed to work harder, pick more cotton, carry bigger rocks, swing a hammer faster. Whatever us slaves had to do, I was supposed to do it better. But I never liked being told what to do. Mister Prater, he was the master, liked to watch me wrestle other men. Other slaves. If I lost, I got whipped. I only lost once."

"Your back ..." I began, thinking there was no way all those scars were from one whipping.

"The overseer, Mister Avery, was scared of me. He was the meanest man I've ever seen. He whipped my mama in the field one day because her cotton sack fell off her shoulder and spilled some cotton," Jerome said. "Just spilled it. All she had to do was pick it up off the ground. He called her a lazy nigger bitch and cracked his whip on her back." Jerome stopped and took several deep breaths. "I dragged him right off his horse and I beat the hell out of him. All the other slaves, they stood around and watched. They were so shocked they just stood there with their mouths hanging open while Mama kept telling me to stop." He paused, and his brown eyes were looking far back. "I damn near killed him."

I felt like I should say something, but there was nothing to say.

"Mister Prater ordered one hundred lashes for that," Jerome went on. "Everyone thought it would kill me, and it almost did. It was more than a week before I could put on a shirt. He sold my mama to somebody buying up slaves to work in Alabama. One day she was there taking care of my back, and then she was gone. Eventually, I had to get up, get dressed, and go back to work. There was a new overseer, just as mean. The only difference was Mama was gone."

Jerome looked up at me at last and I could see the tracks of tears reflecting the firelight back at me. His eyes were wet and glassy. "Then the war ended and we were all free. Mister Prater and the other white folks, they locked themselves up in their fancy houses and pointed guns out the windows and told us to get our black asses off their property. I left. I learned to use guns and I became a bounty hunter. Like you see now."

I nodded.

"There's a reason I'm telling you this, young Jake," he said. "I could go back and find Prater and Avery and I could kill them for what they did to me and what they did to my mama. You've seen the scars now. Does your heart look like that?"

I couldn't answer that.

"They'd hang me sure if I went and killed those white men," Jerome went on. "I couldn't make a future if I held on to the past. I didn't want to let it go. I dream about killing them. I see them in the sights of my gun and I pull the trigger four, five times a week. But I know if I do it for real, I'm giving up everything else I might ever have." He looked at me hard, expecting a response.

"I understand," I said. "I'm sorry."

"I don't want you to be sorry, Jake," he said. "I want you to decide right here in this camp, tonight, if you're gonna die for your past or live for your future. If you choose death, then we're finished. I won't trust my life to a partner that's ready to die. I'll only keep you if I know you're gonna fight tooth and nail to live. You decide tonight. If you're still here in the morning, I'll know. Good night."

Without waiting for any kind of response from me, he threw himself into his bedroll, pulled up the blanket and pulled the brim of his big black hat down over his eyes. I sat and poked and stirred the fire, thinking, and soon I heard Jerome softly snoring.

His back ... the image of all those scars wouldn't leave me. And then to have his mother sold. How did he not go and kill the men who'd hurt him? Could they have done anything worse to him? Could they have ...

Having my heart broken by a fickle girl my own mother had warned me about suddenly seemed almost trifling. Was Rebecca Dickenson's withheld love worth dying over? Was my pain worse than Jerome's? I looked at the man and wondered if he was dreaming about the revenge he denied himself right now.

Then I thought about the Jerome I'd come to know. Not the man who spoke so intelligently and with as much depth as any of those old philosophers I'd had to read in school, but the man who grinned and joked and never let something like eating at the back door of a restaurant bother him. He'd endured all that pain, carried all those scars, and yet was happy and loved his life.

Could I be like that?

I pulled the letter from my pocket again and turned it over and over between my fingers as if it was a square wheel. I almost unfolded it to read it one more time, but instead I flicked it from my fingers and into the fire. The pulpy paper caught immediately, flared up with an orange flame that seemed for a moment to be separate from all the other flames as it devoured the new fuel, and then it was nothing but a bit of black ash floating upward toward those stars I'd looked at earlier.

"You done did the right thing, young Jake," Jerome said from under his hat, his voice back to the joyful country accent I'd been used to.

"Go to sleep, you tricky old bastard," I told him.

"Mmm. We ride for the Territory in the mornin', young Jake. They's bad men to ketch and money to make," Jerome said.

ALSO BY

The Werewolf Saga

Shara

Ulrik

Nadia's Children
First Born (coming soon)
The Werewolf Saga: Apocrypha

Call to the Hunt

Murdered by Human Wolves
Cody Treat Series

Afterlife
The Saga of Tarod the Nine-Fingered

The War Lord

The Puppet King

The Teacher

Yes or No
<u>With Carrie Jones</u>
After Obsession
In the Woods
Sleeper (coming soon)
<u>Short Story Collections</u>
Darkscapes (third edition coming soon)

The God of Discord and Other Weird Tales

The Zombie Whisperer and Other Weird Tales

Unholy Womb and Other Halloween Tales
<u>Non-Fiction</u>

You Want to Do What? Things I've Learned as a Teacher
<u>As Editor</u>
Tales of the Pack

ABOUT THE AUTHOR

Steven E. Wedel began craving fame and fortune in the literary world when he was in high school. After writing his way through careers as a machinist, journalist, corporate writer, public relations specialist, and finally retiring as a high school English teacher, he's decided to keep writing despite the lack of wealth and notoriety.

Wedel has published over 30 books, mostly in the adult horror genre, but he's also written for the young adult, children's, Western, and thriller markets. He's dabbled in other genres using pseudonyms. His non-fiction writing includes how-to articles for writers, literary criticism, and hundreds of articles for print newspapers and online sites.

In 2004 Wedel earned a master's degree in liberal studies, creative writing emphasis, from the University of Oklahoma. He earned a bachelor's degree in journalism from the University of Central Oklahoma in 1999, and graduated from Enid High School in 1984. He is a lifelong Oklahoman, father of four, with three grandsons. He currently lives in central Oklahoma with his dogs Bear and Sweet Pea, and a cat named Cleo.

He'd still take the fame and fortune if it comes his way ...

Be sure to visit him online and sign up for his newsletter: www.stevenewedel.com

Excerpt from Apache Justice

Book 2 in The Travels of Jacob Wolf

The rain was almost like tiny clubs beating on me as I stood just inside the cover of the cottonwoods growing along the creek. George, off behind me a little, had slightly more shelter from the branches, but the storm had his nerves up and he let me know with snorts and stamps that he didn't want to be here. I couldn't blame him. Water pounded against my black slicker and ran off in sheets while a waterfall cascaded from the brim of my soaked hat. Not far behind George, the creek was nearing the top of its bank and would be over it soon.

My Winchester was held protectively inside my unbuttoned slicker in my right hand while my left held the coat closed. My eyes were fixed on the wrought-iron gates of the Indian school. At any moment, I expected either Jerome Freeman to come out leading Frank Dale, or for Frank Dale to burst through those gates at a dead run. I strained my ears for the sound of gunshots and my soul nearly came out of my body when lightning flashed overhead with the sharp crack of thunder, almost like God Himself had clapped his hands to get my full attention.

For a moment after, there was only the sound of the rain. Then I heard something I couldn't identify. It was a high-pitched, wordless babble of fear and panic. I strained to see where it was coming from, but there was nothing except the high, dark walls of the Indian school where bank robber and murderer Frank Dale had gone to hide.

The lightning flashed again and in the instant of illumination, I saw it all. The gates of the school swung open and dozens of children spilled out. They were kids of all ages, soaked to the skin by the rain, running as if their lives depended on it while a buckskin horse charged through them. As I watched, a child who couldn't be more than five or six years old went under the hooves of the running animal.

On the horse's back was Frank Dale. He wasn't alone. There was another child draped over his saddle before him, and in his left arm he held the small, kicking figure of a nun in a wet, clingy, black-and-white habit.

What had happened? Where was Jerome?

I raised my rifle to my shoulder, the afterimage of horse and rider burned into my vision, but it was too dark to see now. I hoped for another flash of lightning, and I got it just as the buckskin reached the wooden bridge over the creek. The nun fought and squirmed in his grasp while I tried to sight in on where his head should be as the world went dark again.

Thunder crashed, louder than ever, and now there were children streaming past me. George was bellowing in fear behind me. If I missed, might kill the nun, or maybe one of the fleeing children.

Steel-shod hooves thundered over the wooden bridge and Frank Dale got away from us again.